THE BEST
OF PADDINGTON

This edition first published in Great Britain
in 1985 by

Octopus Books Limited
59 Grosvenor Street
London W1

This arrangement © 1985 Octopus Books Limited

© illustrations Peggy Fortnum and William Collins Sons & Co Ltd
1983, 1985

© text Michael Bond 1959, 1964, 1974

A Spot of Decorating, from *More about Paddington*;
Paddington Cleans Up, from *Paddington on Top*;
A Day By the Sea, from *Paddington Marches on.*

ISBN 0 86273 255 7

Produced by
Mandarin Publishers Limited
22a Westlands Road
Quarry Bay, Hong Kong

Printed in Italy

CONTENTS

A Spot of Decorating

Paddington gave a deep sigh and pulled his hat down over his ears in an effort to keep out the noise. There was such a hullabaloo going on it was difficult to write up the notes in his scrapbook.

The excitement had all started when Mr and Mrs Brown and Mrs Bird received an unexpected invitation to a wedding. Luckily both Jonathan and Judy were out for the day or things might have been far worse.

Paddington hadn't been included in the invitation, but he didn't really mind. He didn't like weddings very much — apart from the free cakes — and he'd been promised a piece of that whether he went or not.

All the same, he was beginning to wish everyone would hurry up and go. He had a special reason for wanting to be alone that day.

He sighed again, wiped the pen carefully on the back of his paw, and then mopped up some ink blots which somehow or other had found their way on to the table. He was only just in time, for at that moment the door burst open and Mrs Brown rushed in.

'Ah, there you are, Paddington!' She stopped short in the middle of the room and stared at him. 'Why on earth are you wearing your hat indoors?' she asked. 'And why is your tongue all blue?'

Paddington stuck out his tongue as far as he could. 'It *is* a funny colour,' he admitted, squinting down at it with interest. 'Perhaps I'm sickening for something!'

'You'll be sickening for something all right if you don't clear up this mess,' grumbled Mrs Bird as she entered. 'Just look at it. Bottles of ink. Glue. Bits of paper. My best sewing scissors. Marmalade all over the table runner, and goodness knows what else.'

Paddington looked around. It *was* in a bit of a state.

'I've almost finished,' he announced. 'I've just got to rule a few more lines and things. I've been writing my memories.'

Paddington took his scrapbook very seriously and spent many long hours carefully pasting in pictures and writing up his adventures. Since he'd been at the Browns so much had happened it was now more than half full.

'Well, make sure you *do* clear everything up,' said Mrs Brown, 'or we shan't bring you back any cake. Now do take care of yourself. And don't forget — when the baker comes we want two loaves.' With that she waved good-bye and followed Mrs Bird out of the room.

'You know,' said Mrs Bird, as she stepped into the car, 'I have a feeling that bear has something up his paw. He seemed most anxious for us to leave.'

'Oh, I don't know,' said Mrs Brown. 'I don't see what he *can* do. We shan't be away all that long.'

'Ah!' replied Mrs Bird, darkly. 'That's as may be. But he's been hanging about on the landing upstairs half the morning. I'm sure he's up to something.'

Mr Brown, who didn't like weddings much either, and was secretly wishing he could stay at home with Paddington, looked over his shoulder as he let in the clutch. 'Perhaps I ought to stay as well,' he said. 'Then I could get on with decorating his new room.'

'Now, Henry,' said Mrs Brown, firmly. 'You're coming to the wedding and that's that. Paddington will be quite all right by himself. He's a very capable bear. And as for your wanting to get on with decorating his new room . . . you haven't done a thing towards it for over a fortnight, so I'm sure it can wait another day.'

Paddington's new room had become a sore point in the Brown household. It was over two weeks since Mr Brown had first thought of doing it. So far he had stripped all the old wallpaper from the walls, removed

the picture rails, the wood round the doors, the door handle, and everything else that was loose, or that he had made loose, and bought a lot of bright new wallpaper, some whitewash and some paint. There matters had rested.

In the back of the car Mrs Bird pretended she hadn't heard a thing. An idea had suddenly come into her mind and she was hoping it hadn't entered Paddington's as well; but Mrs Bird knew the workings of Paddington's mind better than most and she feared the worst. Had she but known, her fears were being realised at that very moment. Paddington was busy scratching out the words 'AT A LEWSE END' in his scrapbook and was adding, in large capital letters, the ominous ones: 'DECKERATING MY NEW ROOM!'

It was while he'd been writing 'AT A LEWSE END' in his scrapbook earlier in the day that the idea had come to him. Paddington had noticed in the past that he often got his best ideas when he was 'at a loose end'.

For a long while all his belongings had been packed away ready for the big move to his new room, and he was beginning to get impatient. Every time he wanted anything special he had to undo yards of string and brown paper.

Having underlined the words in red, Paddington cleared everything up, locked his scrapbook carefully in his suitcase, and hurried upstairs. He had several times offered to lend a paw with the decorating, but for some reason or other Mr Brown had put his foot down on the idea and hadn't even allowed him in the room while work was in progress. Paddington couldn't quite understand why. He was sure he would be very good at it.

The room in question was an old box-room which had been out of use for a number of years, and when he entered it, Paddington found it was more interesting than he had expected.

He closed the door carefully behind him and sniffed. There was an exciting smell of paint and whitewash in the air. Not only that, but there were some steps, a trestle table, several brushes, a number of rolls of wallpaper, and a big pail of whitewash.

The room had a lovely echo as well, and he spent a long time sitting in the middle of the floor while he was stirring the paint, just listening to his new voice.

There were so many different and interesting things around that it was a job to know what to do first. Eventually Paddington decided on the painting. Choosing one of Mr Brown's best brushes, he dipped it into the

9

pot of paint and then looked round the room for something to dab it on.

It wasn't until he had been working on the window-frame for several minutes that he began to wish he had started on something else. The brush made his arm ache, and when he tried dipping his paw in the paint pot instead and rubbing it on, more paint seemed to go on to the glass than the wooden part, so that the room became quite dark.

'Perhaps,' said Paddington, waving the brush in the air and addressing the room in general, 'perhaps if I do

the ceiling first with the whitewash I can cover all the drips on the wall with the wallpaper.'

But when Paddington started work on the whitewashing he found it was almost as hard as painting. Even by standing on tip-toe at the very top of the steps, he had a job to reach the ceiling. The bucket of whitewash was much too heavy for him to lift, so that he had to come down the steps every time in order to dip the brush in. And when he carried the brush up again, the whitewash ran down his paw and made his fur all matted.

Looking around him, Paddington began to wish he

was still 'at a loose end'. Things were beginning to get in rather a mess again. He felt sure Mrs Bird would have something to say when she saw it.

It was then that he had a brainwave. Paddington was a resourceful bear and he didn't like being beaten by things. Recently he had become interested in a house which was being built nearby. He had first seen it from the window of his bedroom and since then he'd spent many hours talking to the men and watching while they hoisted their tools and cement up to the top floor by means of a rope and pully. Once, Mr Briggs, the foreman, had even taken him up in the bucket too, and had let him lay several bricks.

Now the Browns' house was an old one and in the middle of the ceiling there was a large hook where a big lamp had once hung. Not only that, but in one corner of the room there was a thin coil of rope as well...

Paddington set to work quickly. First he tied one end of the rope to the handle of the bucket. Then he climbed up the steps and passed the other end through the hook in the ceiling. But even so, when he had climbed down again, it still took him a long time to pull the bucket anywhere near the top of the steps. It was full to the brim with whitewash and very heavy, so that he had to stop

every few seconds and tie the other end of the rope to the steps for safety.

It was when he undid the rope for the last time that things started to go wrong. As Paddington closed his eyes and leaned back for the final pull he suddenly felt to his surprise as if he was floating on air. It was a most strange feeling. He reached out one foot and waved it around. There was definitely nothing there. He opened one eye and then nearly let go of the rope in astonishment as he saw the bucket of whitewash going past him on its way down.

Suddenly everything seemed to happen at once. Before he could even reach out a paw or shout for help, his head hit the ceiling and there was a clang as the bucket hit the floor.

For a few seconds Paddington clung there, kicking the air and not knowing what to do. Then there was a gurgling sound from below. Looking down, he saw to his horror that all the whitewash was running out of the bucket. He felt the rope begin to move again as the bucket got lighter, and then it shot past him again as he descended to land with a bump in the middle of a sea of whitewash.

Even then his troubles weren't over. As he tried to

regain his balance on the slippery floor, he let go of the rope, and with a rushing noise the bucket shot downwards again and landed on top of his head, completely covering him.

Paddington lay on his back in the whitewash for several minutes, trying to get his breath back and wondering what had hit him. When he did sit up and take the bucket off his head he quickly put it back on again. There was whitewash all over the floor, the paint pots had been upset into little rivers of brown and green, and Mr Brown's decorating cap was floating in one corner of the room. When Paddington saw it he felt very glad he'd left *his* hat downstairs.

One thing was certain — he was going to have a lot of explaining to do. And that was going to be even more difficult than usual, because he couldn't even explain to himself quite what had gone wrong.

It was some while later, when he was sitting on the upturned bucket thinking about things, that the idea of doing the wallpapering came to him. Paddington had a hopeful nature and he believed in looking on the bright side. If he did the wallpapering really well, the others might not even notice the mess he'd made.

Paddington was fairly confident about the wallpapering. Unknown to Mr Brown, he had often watched him in the past through a crack in the door, and it looked quite simple. All you had to do was to brush some sticky stuff on the back of the paper and then put it on the wall. The high parts weren't too difficult, even for a bear, because you could fold the paper in two and put a broom in the middle where the fold was. Then you simply pushed the broom up and down the wall in case there were any nasty wrinkles.

Paddington felt much more cheeful now he'd thought of the wallpapering. He found some paste already mixed in another bucket, which he put on top of the trestle while he unrolled the paper. It was a little difficult at first

because every time he tried to unroll the paper he had to crawl along the trestle pushing it with his paws and the other end rolled up again and followed behind him. But eventually he managed to get one piece completely covered in paste.

He climbed down off the trestle, carefully avoiding the worst of the whitewash, which by now was beginning to dry in large lumps, and lifted the sheet of wallpaper on to a broom. It was a long sheet of paper, much longer than it had seemed when he was putting the paste on, and somehow or other, as Paddington waved the broom about over his head, it began to wrap itself around him. After a struggle he managed to push his way out and headed in the general direction of a piece of wall. He stood back and surveyed the result. The paper was torn in several places, and there seemed to be a lot of paste on the outside, but Paddington felt quite pleased with himself. He decided to try another piece, then another, running backwards and forwards between the trestle and the walls as fast as his legs could carry him in an effort to get it all finished before the Browns returned.

Some of the pieces didn't quite join, others overlapped, and on most of them there were some very odd-looking patches of paste and whitewash. None of the pieces were as straight as he would have liked, but when he put his head on one side and squinted, Paddington felt the overall effect was quite nice, and he felt very pleased with himself.

It was as he was taking a final look round the room at his handiwork that he noticed something very strange. There was a window, and there was also a fireplace. But there was no longer any sign of a door. Paddington stopped squinting and his eyes grew rounder and rounder. He distinctly remembered there *had* been a door because he had come through it. He blinked at all four walls. It was difficult to see properly because the paint on the window-glass had started to dry and there was hardly any light coming through — but there most definitely wasn't a door!

'I can't understand it,' said Mr Brown as he entered the dining-room. 'I've looked everywhere and there's no sign of Paddington. I told you I should have stayed at home with him.'

Mrs Brown looked worried. 'Oh dear, I hope nothing's happened to him. It's so unlike him to go out without leaving a note.'

'He's not in his room,' said Judy.

'Mr Gruber hasn't seen him either,' added Jonathan. 'I've just been down to the market and he says he hasn't seen him since they had cocoa together this morning.'

'Have *you* seen Paddington anywhere?' asked Mrs Brown as Mrs Bird entered, carrying a tray of supper things.

'I don't know about Paddington,' said Mrs Bird. 'I've been having enough trouble over the water pipes without missing bears. I think they've got an air lock or something. They've been banging away every since we came in.'

Mr Brown listened for a moment. 'It *does* sound like water pipes,' he said. 'And yet . . . it isn't regular enough, somehow.' He went outside into the hall. 'It's a sort of thumping noise. . .'

'Crikey!' shouted Jonathan. 'Listen . . . it's someone

sending an S.O.S.'

Everyone exchanged glances and then, in one voice cried: 'Paddington!'

'Mercy me,' said Mrs Bird as they burst through the papered-up door. 'There must have been an earthquake or something. And either that's Paddinton or it's his ghost!' She pointed towards a small, white figure as it rose from an upturned bucket to greet them.

'I couldn't find the door,' said Paddington, plaintively. 'I think I must have papered it over when I came in. I remember seeing it. So I banged on the floor with a broom handle.'

'Gosh!' said Jonathan, admiringly. 'What a mess!'

'You ... papered ... it ... over ... when ... you ... did ... the ... decorating,' repeated Mr Brown. He was a bit slow to grasp things sometimes.

'That's right,' said Paddington. 'I did it as a surprise.' He waved a paw round the room. 'I'm afraid it's in a bit of a mess, but it isn't dry yet.'

While the idea was slowly sinking into Mr Brown's mind, Mrs Bird came to Paddington's rescue. 'Now it's not a bit of good holding an inquest,' she said. 'What's done is done. And if you ask me it's a good thing too. Now perhaps we shall get some proper decorators in to

do the job.' With that she took hold of Paddington's paw and led him out of the room.

'As for you, young bear — you're going straight into a hot bath before all the plaster stuff sets hard!'

Mr Brown looked after the retreating figures of Mrs Bird and Paddington and then at the long trail of white footprints and pawmarks. 'Bears!' he said, bitterly.

Paddington hung about in his room for a long time after his bath and waited until the last possible minute before going downstairs to supper. He had a nasty feeling he was in disgrace. But surprisingly the word

'decorating' wasn't mentioned at all that evening.

Even more surprisingly, while he was sitting up in bed drinking his cocoa, several people came to see him and each of them gave him a sixpence. It was all very mysterious, but Paddington didn't like to ask why in case they changed their minds.

It was Judy who solved the problem for him when she came in to say good night.

'I expect Mummy and Mrs Bird gave you sixpence because they don't want Daddy to do any more decorating,' she explained. 'He always starts things and never finishes them. And I expect Daddy gave you one because he didn't want to finish it anyway. Now they're getting a proper decorator in, so everyone's happy!'

Paddington sipped his cocoa thoughtfully. 'Perhaps if I did another room I'd get another one and sixpence,' he said.

'Oh, no, you don't,' said Judy sternly. 'You've done quite enough for one day. If I were you I shouldn't mention the word "decorating" for a long time to come.'

'Perhaps you're right,' said Paddington sleepily, as he stretched out his paws. 'But I *was* at a loose end.'

Paddington Cleans Up

Paddington peered through the letter-box at number thirty-two Windsor Gardens with a look of surprise on his face.

In point of fact he'd been watching out for the postman, but instead of the blue-grey uniform he'd hoped to see, Mr Curry, the Browns' next-door neighbour had loomed into view. Mr Curry looked as if he was in a bad temper. He was never at his best in the morning, but even through the half-open flap it was plain to see he was in an even worse mood than usual. He was shaking a rug over the pavement, and from the cloud of dust surrounding him it looked as though he had been cleaning out his grate and had just had a nasty accident with the ashes.

The expression on his face boded ill for anyone who happened to come within his range of vision, and it was unfortunate that his gaze alighted on the Browns' front door at the very moment when Paddington opened the letter-box.

'Bear!' he bellowed. 'How dare you spy on me like that? I've a very good mind to report you!'

Paddington let go of the flap as if it had been resting in hot coals, and gazed at the closed door with a very disappointed air indeed. Apart from an occasional catalogue he didn't get many letters, but all the same he always looked forward to seeing the postman arrive, and he felt most aggrieved at being deprived of his morning's treat, especially as he'd been half-expecting a postcard from his Aunt Lucy in Peru. Something she'd said when she'd last written had given him food for thought and he was anxiously awaiting the next instalment.

All the same, he knew better than to get on the wrong side of Mr Curry, so he decided to forget the matter and pay his daily visit to the nearby market in the Portobello Road instead.

A few minutes later, having taken his shopping basket

on wheels from the cupboard under the stairs, he collected Mrs Bird's shopping list, made sure the coast was clear, and set out on his journey.

Over the years Paddington's basket on wheels had become a familiar sight in the market, and it was often much admired by passers-by. Paddington took great care of it. He'd several times varnished the basketwork, and the wheels were kept so well oiled there was never a squeak. Earlier in the year Mr Brown had bought him two new tyres, so all in all it still looked as good as new.

After he'd completed Mrs Bird's shopping, Paddington called in at the baker's for his morning supply of buns. Then he carried on down the Portobello Road in order to visit the antique shop belonging to his friend, Mr Gruber.

Paddington liked visiting Mr Gruber. Apart from selling antiques, Mr Gruber possessed a large number of books, and although no one knew if he'd actually read them all, it certainly seemed as though he must have, for he was a mine of information on almost every subject one could think of.

When he arrived he found Mr Gruber sitting on the horsehair sofa just inside his shop clutching a particularly large volume.

'You'll never guess what today's book is about, Mr Brown,' he said, holding it up for Paddington to see. 'It's called "Diseases of the Cocoa Bean", and there are over seven hundred and fifty pages.'

Paddington's face grew longer and longer as he listened to Mr Gruber recite from the long list of things that could happen to a cocoa bean before it actually reached the shops. He always rounded off his morning excursions with a visit to his friend, and Mr Gruber's contribution to the meeting was a never-ending supply of cocoa, which he kept at the ready on a small stove at the back of the shop. It didn't seem possible that this could ever come to an end.

'Perhaps we'd better get some more stocks in, Mr Gruber,' he exclaimed anxiously, when there was a gap in the conversation.

Mr Gruber smiled. 'I don't think there's any risk of our going short yet awhile, Mr Brown,' he replied, as he busied himself at the stove. 'But I think it does go to show how we tend to take things for granted. We very rarely get something for nothing in this world.'

Paddington looked slightly relieved at Mr Gruber's reassuring words. All the same, it was noticeable that he sipped his cocoa even more slowly than usual, and when he'd finished he carefully wiped round his mug with the remains of a bun in order to make sure he wasn't letting any go to waste.

Even after he'd said goodbye to Mr Gruber he still had a very thoughtful expression on his face. In fact, his mind was so far away it wasn't until he rounded a corner leading into Windsor Gardens that he suddenly came back to earth with a bump as he realised that while he'd been in the shop someone had pinned a note to his shopping basket.

It was short and to the point. It said:

YOUR SHOPPING BASKET ON WHEELS IS IN SUCH GOOD CONDITION IT SHOWS YOU HAVE CHARACTER, DRIVE AND AMBITION. THIS MEANS YOU ARE JUST THE KIND OF PERSON WE ARE LOOKING FOR. YOU COULD EARN £100 PER WEEK WITH NO MORE EFFORT THAN IT TAKES TO VISIT THE GROCERS. I WILL BE IN TOUCH SOON WITH FURTHER DETAILS.

It was written in large capital letters and it was signed YOURS TRULY. A WELL-WISHER.

Paddington read the note several times. He could hardly believe his eyes. Only a moment before he'd been racking his brains to think up ways of earning some extra money so that he could buy Mr Gruber a tin or two of cocoa; and now, out of nowhere, came this strange offer. It couldn't have happened at a better moment, especially as he'd been tempted to break into the savings which he kept in the secret compartment of his suitcase, and which he held in reserve for important occasions, like birthdays and Christmas.

It was hard to believe he could earn so much money simply because he'd kept his shopping basket clean, but before he had chance to consider the matter he saw a man in a fawn raincoat approaching. The man was carrying a large cardboard box which seemed to contain something heavy, for as he drew near he rested it on Paddington's basket while he paused in order to mop his brow.

He looked Paddington up and down for a moment and then held out his hand. 'Just as I thought!' he exclaimed. 'It's nice when you have a picture of someone in your mind and they turn out exactly as you expected. I'm glad you got my note. If you don't mind me saying so, sir, you should go far.'

Paddington held out his paw in return. 'Thank you,

Mr Wisher,' he replied. 'But I don't think I shall go very far this morning. I'm on my way home.' He gave the man a hard stare. Although he was much too polite to say so, he couldn't really return the man's compliments. From the tone of the letter he'd expected someone rather superior, whereas his new acquaintance looked more than a trifle seedy.

Catching sight of Paddington's glance, the man hastily pulled his coat sleeves down over his cuffs. 'I must apologise for my appearance,' he said. 'But I've got rid of ... er, I've obtained so many new clients for my vacuum cleaners this morning I don't know whether I'm coming or going. I haven't even had time to go home and change.'

'Your *vacuum cleaners!*' exclaimed Paddington in surprise.

The man nodded. 'I must say, sir,' he continued, 'it's your lucky day. It just so happens that you've caught me with my very last one. Until I take delivery of a new batch later on, of course,' he added hastily.

Taking a quick glance over his shoulder, he produced a piece of pasteboard, which he held up in front of Paddington's eyes for a fleeting moment before returning it to an inside pocket.

'My card,' he announced. 'Just to show that all's above board and Sir Garnet like.

'You, too, could become a member of our happy band and make yourself a fortune. Every new member gets, free of charge, our latest model cleaner, *and* . . . for today only, a list of dos and don'ts for making your very first sale.

'Now,' he slapped the box to emphasise his point, 'I'm not asking twenty pounds for this very rare privilege. I'm not asking fifteen. I'm not even asking ten. To you, because I like the look of your face, and because I think you're just the sort of bear we are looking for, *two* pounds!'

His voice took on a confidential tone. 'If I was to tell you the names of some of the people I've sold cleaners to you probably wouldn't believe me. But I won't bore you with details like that. You're probably asking yourself what you have to do in order to earn all this money, right? Well, I'll tell you.

'You sell this cleaner for four pounds, right? You then buy two more cleaners for two pounds each and sell *them* for four, making twelve pounds in all, right? Then you either keep the money or you buy six more cleaners and sell those. If you work hard you'll make a fortune so fast

31

you won't even have time to get to the bank.

'Another thing you may be asking yourself,' he continued, before Paddington had time to say anything, 'is why anyone who already has a vacuum cleaner should buy one of ours?'

He gave the box another slap. 'Never fear, it's all in here. Ask no questions, tell no lies. With our new cleaner you can suck up anything. Dirt, muck, ashes, soot . . . pile it all on, anything you like. A flick of the switch and whoosh, it'll disappear in a flash.

'But,' he warned, 'you'll have to hurry. I've a queue of customers waiting round the next corner.'

Paddington needed no second bidding. It wasn't every day such an offer came his way, and he felt sure he would be able to buy an awful lot of cocoa for twelve pounds. Hurrying behind a nearby car he bent down and opened his suitcase.

'Thank you very much,' said the man, as Paddington counted out two crisp one pound notes. 'Sorry I can't stop, guv, but work calls . . .'

Paddington had been about to enquire where he could pick up his next lot of cleaners, but before he had a chance to open his mouth the man had disappeared.

For a moment he didn't know what to do. He felt very

tempted to take the cleaner straight indoors in order to test it in his bedroom, but he wasn't at all sure Mrs Bird would approve. In any case, number thirty-two Windsor Gardens was always kept so spotlessly clean there didn't seem much point.

And then, as he reached the end of the road, the matter was suddenly decided for him. Mr Curry's front door shot open and the Browns' neighbour emerged once again carrying a dustpan and brush.

He glanced at Paddington. 'Are you still spying on me, bear?' he growled. 'I've told you about it once before this morning.'

'Oh, no, Mr Curry,' said Paddington hastily. 'I'm not spying on anyone. I've got a job. I'm selling a special new cleaner.'

Mr Curry looked at Paddington uncertainly. 'Is this true, bear?' he demanded.

'Oh, yes,' said Paddington. 'It gets rid of anything. I can give you a free demonstration if you like.'

A sly gleam entered Mr Curry's eyes. 'As a matter of fact,' he said, 'it does so happen that I'm having a spot of bother this morning. I'm not saying I'll buy anything mind, but if you care to clear up the mess I *might* consider it.'

Paddington consulted the handwritten list of instructions which was pinned to the box. He could see that Mr Curry was going to come under the heading of CUSTOMERS — VERY DIFFICULT.

'I think,' he announced, as the Browns' neighbour helped him up the step with his basket on wheels, 'you're going to need what we call the "full treatment"'.

Mr Curry gave a snort. 'It had better be good, bear,' he said. 'Otherwise I shall hold you personally responsible.'

He led the way into his dining-room and pointed to a large pile of black stuff in the grate. 'I've had a bad fall of soot this morning. Probably to do with the noise that goes on next door,' he added meaningfully.

'My cleaner's very good with soot, Mr Curry,' said Paddington eagerly. 'Mr Wisher mentioned it specially.'

'Good,' said Mr Curry. 'I'll just go and finish emptying my dustpan and then I'll be back to keep an eye on things.'

As the Browns' neighbour disappeared from view Paddington hurriedly set to work. Remembering the advice he'd been given a short while before, he decided to make certain he gave Mr Curry a very good demonstration indeed.

Grabbing hold of a broom which was standing nearby, he quickly brushed the soot into a large pile in the middle of the hearth. Then he poked the broom up the chimney and waved it around several times. His hopes were speedily realised. There was a rushing sound and a moment later an even bigger load of soot landed at his feet. Ignoring the black clouds which were beginning to fill the room, Paddington removed the cardboard box from his basket, and examined Mrs Bird's shopping. As he'd feared, some of it had suffered rather badly under the weight and he added the remains of some broken custard tarts, several squashed tomatoes, and a number of cracked eggs to the pile.

It was while he was stirring it all up with the handle of the broom that Mr Curry came back into the room. For a moment he stood as if transfixed.

'Bear!' he bellowed. 'Bear! What on earth do you think you're doing?'

Paddington stood up and gazed at his handiwork. Now that he was viewing it from a distance he had to admit it *was* rather worse than he had intended.

'It's all part of my demonstration, Mr Curry,' he explained, with more confidence than he felt.

'Now,' he said, putting on his best salesman's voice as he consulted the instructions again, 'I'm sure you will agree that no ordinary cleaner would be any good with this mess.'

For once in his life it seemed that Mr Curry was in complete and utter accord with Paddington. 'Have you taken leave of your senses, bear?' he spluttered.

Paddington gave the cardboard box a slap. 'No, Mr Curry,' he exclaimed. 'Never fear, it's all in here. Ask no questions, I'll tell no lies.'

Mr Curry looked as if there were a good many questions he was only too eager to ask, but instead he pointed a trembling finger at the box.

'Never fear, it's all in here!' he bellowed. 'It had better all be in there! If it's not all in there within thirty seconds I shall ...'

Mr Curry paused for breath, suddenly at a loss for words.

Taking advantage of the moment, Paddington opened the lid of the box and withdrew a long piece of wire with a plug on the end.

He peered at the skirting board. 'Can you tell me

where your socket is, Mr Curry?' he enquired.

If Paddington had asked the Browns' neighbour for the loan of a million pounds he couldn't have had a more unfavourable reaction. Mr Curry's face, which had been growing redder and redder with rage, suddenly went a deep shade of purple as he gazed at the object in Paddington's paw.

'My socket?' he roared. '*My socket*? I haven't any sockets, bear! I don't even have any electricity. I use gas!'

Paddington's jaw dropped, and the plug slipped from his paw and fell unheeded to the floor as he gazed at the Browns' neighbour. If Mr Curry's face had gone a deep shade of purple, Paddington's — or the little that could be seen of it beneath his fur — was as white as a sheet.

He wasn't sure what happened next. He remembered Mr Curry picking up the cardboard box as if he was about to hurl it through the window, but he didn't wait to see any more. He dashed out through the front door and back into number thirty-two Windsor Gardens as if his very life depended on it.

To his surprise the door was already open, but it wasn't until he cannoned into Mr Gruber that he discovered the reason why. His friend was deep in conversation with the other members of the family.

For some reason they seemed even more pleased to see him than he was to see them.

'There you are!' exclaimed Mrs Bird.

'Thank goodness,' said Mrs Brown thankfully.

'Are you all right?' chorused Jonathan and Judy.

'I think so,' gasped Paddington, peering over his shoulder as he hastily closed the door behind him.

'No one's tried to sell you a vacuum cleaner?' asked Mrs Bird.

Paddington stared at the Browns' housekeeper in amazement. It really was uncanny the way Mrs Bird 'knew' about things.

'There have been some "goings-on" down at the market this morning, Mr Brown,' broke in Mr Gruber. 'That's why I popped in. Someone's been selling dud vacuum cleaners and when I heard you'd been seen talking to him I began to get worried.'

'When you were so late back we thought something might have happened to you,' said Mrs Brown.

'Well,' said Paddington vaguely, 'I think it has!'

Paddington launched into his explanations. It was a bit difficult, partly because he wasn't too sure how to put some of it into words, but also because there was a good

39

deal of noise going on outside. Shouts and bangs, and the sound of a loud argument, followed a moment or so later by the roar of a car drawing away.

'Fancy trying to take advantage of someone like that,' said Mrs Bird grimly, when Paddington had finished.

'He seemed quite a nice man, Mrs Bird,' said Paddington.

'I didn't mean the vacuum cleaner salesman,' said Mrs Bird. 'At least he gave you *something* for your money — even if it didn't work. I meant Mr Curry. He's always after something for nothing.'

'He's too mean to get his chimney swept for a start,' said Judy.

'And I bet he's still waiting to see if electricity catches on before he changes over,' agreed Jonathan.

They broke off as the telephone started to ring and Mrs Bird hurried across the hall to answer it.

'Yes,' she said after a moment. 'Really? Yes, of course. Well, we'll do our best,' she added after a while, 'but it may not be for some time. Probably later on this morning.'

The others grew more and more mystified as they listened to their end of the conversation.

'What on earth was all that about?' asked Mrs Brown,

as her housekeeper replaced the receiver.

'It seems,' said Mrs Bird gravely, 'that the police think they may have caught the man who's selling the dud vacuum cleaners. They want someone to go down and identify him.'

'Oh, dear,' said Mrs Brown. 'I don't really like the idea of Paddington being involved in things like that.'

'Who said anything about Paddington?' asked Mrs Bird innocently. 'Anyway, I suggest we all have a nice hot drink before we do anything else. There's no point in rushing things.'

The others exchanged glances as they followed Mrs Bird into the kitchen. She could be very infuriating at times. But the Browns' housekeeper refused to be drawn, and it wasn't until they were all settled round the kitchen table with their second lot of elevenses that she brought the matter up again.

'It seems,' she mused, 'that the man they arrested was caught right outside our house. He was carrying a cleaner at the time. He said his name was Murray, or Hurry or something like that ... Anyway, he insists we know him.'

'Crumbs!' exclaimed Jonathan as light began to dawn. 'Don't say they picked on Mr Curry by mistake!'

'I bet that's what all the row was about just now,' said Judy. 'I bet he was coming round here to complain!'

'Which is why,' said Mrs Bird, when all the excitement had died down, 'I really think it might be better if Paddington doesn't go down to the Police station. It might be rubbing salt into the wound.'

'I quite agree,' said Mr Gruber. 'In fact while you're gone perhaps young Mr Brown and I can go next door and clear up some of the mess.'

'Bags we help too,' Jonathan and Judy eagerly.

All eyes turned to Paddington, who was savouring his drink with even more relish than usual. What with Mr Gruber's book on diseases and the disastrous events in Mr Curry's house he'd almost begun to wonder if he would ever have elevenses again.

'I think,' he announced, as he clasped the mug firmly between his paws, 'I shall never take my cocoa for granted again!'

A Day by the Sea

Mr Brown stood at the open front door of number thirty-two Windsor Gardens and surveyed the morning sun peeping over the top of the houses opposite.

'Hands up all those in favour of a trip to the sea,' he called, looking back over his shoulder.

'People who ask questions like that must expect trouble,' said Mrs Brown, after the hubbub had died down and the last three pairs of feet disappeared hastily up the stairs as their owners went to pack.

'I notice you and Mrs Bird didn't put up your hands, Mary,' said Mr Brown, looking rather hurt. 'I can't think why.'

'I've been on your trips before, Henry,' replied Mrs Brown ominously. 'It usually takes me a week to get over them.'

'And some of us have all the sandwiches to cut,' said Mrs Bird pointedly.

'Sandwiches?' echoed Mr Brown. 'Who said anything about sandwiches?' He waved his hand grandly in the air. 'We'll have lunch in a restaurant. Hang the expense. It's a long time since we had a day out.'

'Well,' said Mrs Brown doubtfully. 'Don't say I didn't warn you.'

Anything else she might have been about to say was lost as another clatter of pounding feet heralded the arrival back downstairs of Jonathan, Judy and Paddington together with all their belongings. Paddington in particular seemed to be very well laden. Apart from his suitcase and hat, which he was wearing as usual, he was also carrying his special seaside straw hat, a beach ball, a rubber bathing ring and a bucket and spade, together

with a windmill on the end of a stick, a pair of binoculars and an assortment of maps.

Mrs Brown gazed at the collection. 'I'm sure they didn't have all this trouble on the Everest expedition,' she exclaimed.

'I don't suppose they took any bears with them,' replied Mrs Bird. 'That's why. And I'm sure they didn't leave a trail of last year's sand on their stairs before they left.'

Paddington looked most upset as he peered out from behind his bucket and listened to the remarks. He was a great believer in being prepared for any kind of emergency and from what he could remember of previous trips to the seaside all sorts of things could happen and usually did.

'Come along everyone,' called Mr Brown, hurriedly coming to his rescue. 'If we don't make an early start we shall get caught up in the rush and then we shall never get there. A day at the sea will do us all good. It'll help blow some of the cobwebs out of your whiskers, Paddington.'

Paddington pricked up his ears. 'Blow some of the cobwebs out of my whiskers, Mr Brown?' he exclaimed, looking even more upset as he followed the others out to the waiting car.

While Jonathan, Judy and Mr Brown packed the equipment into the boot, and Mrs Brown and Mrs Bird went upstairs to change, Paddington stood on the front seat of the car and peered anxiously at his face in the driving mirror. There were several pieces of cotton stuck to his whiskers, not to mention some old marmalade and cocoa stains, but he couldn't see any signs of a spider let alone a cobweb.

Paddington was unusally silent on the journey down and he was still pondering over the matter later that morning when they swept over the brow of a hill and began the long descent towards Brightsea. But as they drew near the front the smell of the sea air and the sight of all the holidaymakers strolling along the promenade soon drove all other thoughts from his mind.

Paddington was very keen on outings, especially Mr Brown's unexpected seaside ones, and he stuck his head out of the front window of the car and peered round excitedly as they drove along the front looking for somewhere to park.

'All hands on deck,' said Mr Brown, as he backed the car into a vacant space. 'Stand by to unload.'

Paddington gathered his belongings and jumped out

on to the pavement. 'I'll find a place on the beach, Mr Brown,' he called eagerly.

In the back of the car Mrs Brown and Mrs Bird exchanged glances.

'I know one thing,' said Mrs Brown, as she helped Mrs Bird out of the car. 'They might not have had any bears with them on the Everest expedition but at least they had some Sherpas to help with their luggage. Just look at it all!'

'It won't take a minute, Mary,' puffed Mr Brown from behind a pile of carrier bags. 'Where's Paddington? He said he'd find a spot for us.'

'There he is,' said Jonathan, pointing to a patch of sand where six deck chairs were already ranged in a row. 'He's talking to that man with the ticket machine.'

'Oh, dear,' said Mrs Brown anxiously. 'He looks rather upset. I hope there's nothing wrong.'

'Trust Paddington to get into trouble,' said Judy. 'We haven't been here a minute.'

The Browns hurried down some steps leading to the beach and as they did so a familiar voice reached their ears.

'Three shillings!' exclaimed the voice bitterly. 'Three shillings just to sit in a deck chair!'

'No, mate,' came the voice of the ticket man in reply. 'It's not three shillings just to sit in a deck chair. You've got six chairs 'ere and they're sixpence each. Six sixes is thirty-six.'

Paddington looked more and more upset as he listened to the man's words. He'd felt very pleased with himself when he'd found the pile of chairs beside a patch of clean sand but almost before he'd had time to arrange them in a row, and certainly before he'd had a chance to test even one of them, the man had appeared as if by magic from behind a beach hut, waving his ticket machine as he pounced on him.

'Three shillings!' he repeated, collapsing into the nearest chair.

'I know your sort,' lectured the man in a loud voice as he looked around and addressed the rest of the beach. 'You sit down in them chairs and pretend you're asleep

when I comes round for the money. Or else you say yer tickets 'ave blowed away. Your sort cost the Corporation 'undreds of pounds a year.'

The man's voice trailed away as a muffled cry came from somewhere near his feet.

''Ere,' he exclaimed, as he bent down and stared at a heaving mass of striped canvas. 'What's 'appened?'

'Help!' came the muffled voice again.

'Dear, oh dear,' said the man as he disentangled Paddington from the chair. 'You couldn't have 'ad yer back strut properly adjusted.'

'My back strut!' exclaimed Paddington, sitting up.

'That's right,' said the man. 'You're supposed to fit it into the slots — not just rest it on the side. No wonder it collapsed.'

Paddington gave the man a hard stare as he scrambled to his feet and undid his suitcase. Sixpence seemed a lot to pay just to sit in a chair at the best of times, but when it didn't even have any instructions and collapsed into the bargain, words failed him.

'Instructions?' echoed the man, as he took Paddington's money and rang up six tickets. 'I've never 'eard of a deck chair 'aving instructions before. You wants a lot for yer money.'

'I hope you haven't been having any trouble,' said Mr Brown, as he hurried on to the scene and pressed something round and shiny into the man's hand.

'Trouble?' said the ticket man, his expression changing as he felt the coin. 'Bless you no, sir. Just a slight misunderstanding as yer might say. Tell you what, guv,' he continued, turning to Paddington and touching his cap with a more respectful air. 'I know these days out at the seaside can come pretty expensive for a young bear gent what's standing a treat. If you wants to get yer money back and make a profit into the bargain your best plan is to keep a weather eye open for Basil Budd.'

'Basil Budd?' repeated Paddington, looking most surprised.

'That's right,' said the man, pointing towards a large

notice pasted on the sea wall. 'He's in Brightsea today. It's one of them newspaper stunts. The first one as confronts 'im and says "You're Basil Budd" gets five pounds reward. Only mind you're carrying one of his newspapers,' he warned. 'Otherwise 'e won't pay up.'

So saying, he touched his cap once more and hurried off up the beach in the direction of some new arrivals, leaving the Browns to arrange themselves and their belongings on Paddington's patch of sand.

Mr Brown turned to thank Paddington for standing treat with the deck chairs but already he had disappeared up the sand and was standing gazing at the poster on the sea wall with a thoughtful expression on his face.

The poster had the one word SENSATION written in large, red capital letters across the top. Underneath was a picture of a man in a trilby hat followed by the announcement that Basil Budd of the *Daily Globe* was in town.

The smaller print which followed went on to explain all that the deck-chair man had told them. It took Paddington some while to read all the poster, particularly as he read some of the more interesting bits several times in case he'd made a mistake. But whichever way he read the notice it seemed that not only was Basil Budd

anxious to give away five pound notes to anyone who confronted him, but that his own seaside outing would be ruined if he had so much as one note left at the end of the day.

'Good Heaveans!' said Mr Brown, as he glanced up the beach again. 'Paddington *is* lashing out today. He's bought himself a newspaper now!'

'I pity the person who happens to look anything like Basil Budd,' said Mrs Bird. 'I can see there'll be some nasty scenes if they don't pay up.'

Mr Brown wriggled into his costume. 'Come on, Paddington,' he called. 'It's time for a bathe.'

After taking one last look at the poster Paddington turned and came slowly back down the beach. Although he'd been looking forward all the morning to a paddle he was beginning to have second thoughts on the matter. Paddington liked dipping his paws in the sea as much as anyone but he didn't want to run the risk of missing five pounds reward if Basil Budd happened to stroll by while his back was turned.

'Perhaps he's having a paddle himself,' said Mrs Bird helpfully.

Paddington brightened at the thought. He took out his opera glasses and peered through them at the figures already in the water. There didn't seem to be any sign of a man wearing a trilby hat, but all the same a moment later he climbed into his rubber bathing ring and hurried down to the water's edge clutching the copy of the *Daily Globe* in one paw and his suitcase in the other.

Mrs Bird sighed. Paddington was just too far away for her to make out the expression on his face, but she didn't at all like the look of the little she could see. From where she was sitting some of the stares he was giving passers-by seemed very hard ones indeed.

'Why can't we have a nice quiet day at the sea like any normal family?' she said.

'At least it keeps him out of mischief,' replied Mrs Brown. 'And we know where he is which is something.'

'That's not going to last very long,' said Mrs Bird, ominously, as she watched Paddington splash his way along the shore in the direction of the pier. 'There's plenty of time yet. You mark my words.'

Unaware of the anxious moments he was causing, Paddington plodded on his way, pausing every now and then to compare the picture on the front page of his paper with that of a passer-by.

The beach was beginning to fill up. There were fat men in shorts, thin men in bathing costumes, men of all shapes and sizes; some wore sun hats, some caps, others coloured hats made of cardboard, and once he even saw a man wearing a bowler, but as far as he could make out there wasn't one person along the whole of the Brightsea front who bore any resemblance to Basil Budd.

After making his way along the beach for the third time Paddington stopped by the pier and mopped his brow while he took another long look at a *Daily Globe* poster.

It was a strange thing but somehow with each journey up and down the beach the expression on Basil Budd's face seemed to change. At first it had been quite an ordinary, pleasant sort of face, but now that he looked at it more closely Paddington decided there was a mocking air about it which he didn't like the look of at all.

With a sigh he found himself a quiet corner of the beach and sat down with his back against a pile of deck chairs in order to consider the matter. Taken all round he was beginning to feel very upset at the way things were going. In fact, if he could have found the man who had sold him the newspaper he would have asked for his money back. But with every minute more and more people were streaming into Brightsea and the chances of finding the newspaper seller, let alone Basil Budd himself, seemed more and more remote.

As he sat there deep in thought Paddington's eyelids began to feel heavier and heavier. Several times he pushed them open with a paw but gradually the combination of a large breakfast, several ice-creams, and all the walks up and down the sand in the hot sun, not to mention the distant sound of waves breaking on the sea shore, grew too much for him, and a short while later some gentle snores added themselves to the general hubbub all around.

Mrs Brown heaved a sigh of relief. 'Thank goodness!' she exclaimed, as a small brown figure came hurrying along the promenade towards them. 'I was beginning to think something had happened to him.'

Mr Brown removed his belongings from the only remaining chair at their table. 'About time too,' he grumbled. 'I'm starving.'

In order to avoid the crowds the Browns had arranged to meet for a early lunch on the terrace of a large Brightsea promenade hotel, and all the family with the exception of Paddington had arrived there in good time.

Paddington had a habit of disappearing on occasions, but very rarely at meal times, and as the minutes ticked by and the other tables started to fill up the Browns had become more and more worried.

'Where on earth have you been?' asked Mrs Brown, as Paddington drew near.

Paddington raised his hat with a distant expression on his face. 'I was having a bit of a dream, Mrs Brown,' he replied vaguely.

'A dream?' echoed Mrs Bird. 'I should have thought you had plenty of time for those at home.'

'This was a special seaside one, Mrs Bird,' explained Paddington, looking slightly offended. 'It was very unusual.'

'It must have been,' said Judy, 'if it made you late for lunch.'

Mr Brown handed Paddington a large menu. 'We've ordered you some soup to be going on with,' he said. 'Perhaps you'd like to choose what you want to follow ...'

The Browns looked across at Paddington with some concern. He seemed to be acting most strangely. One moment he'd been about to sit down quietly in his chair, the next moment he had jumped up again and was

peering through his opera glasses with an air of great excitement.

'Is anything the matter?' asked Mr Brown.

Paddington adjusted his glasses. 'I think that's Basil Budd,' he exclaimed, pointing towards a man at the next table.

'Basil Budd?' echoed Mrs Brown. 'But it can't be. He's got a beard.'

'Basil Budd hasn't,' said Jonathan. 'I've seen his picture on the posters.'

Paddington looked even more mysterious. 'That's what my dream was about,' he said. 'Only I don't think it was a dream after all. I'm going to confront him!'

'Oh, dear,' said Mrs Brown nervously, as Paddington stood up. 'Do you think you should?'

But her words fell on deaf ears for Paddington was already tapping the beard man on his shoulder. 'I'd like my five pounds, please, Mr Budd,' he announced, holding up his copy of the *Daily Globe*.

The man paused with a soup spoon halfway to his mouth. 'No, thank you,' he said, looking at the newspaper. 'I've got one already.'

'I'm not a newspaper bear,' said Paddington patiently 'I think you're Basil Budd of the *Daily Globe* and I've come to confront you.'

'You've come to confront me?' repeated the man, as if in a dream. 'But my name isn't Budd. I've never even heard of him.'

Paddington took a deep breath and gave the man the hardest stare he could manage. 'If you don't give me my five pounds,' he exclaimed hotly. 'I shall call a policeman!'

The man returned Paddington's stare with one almost as hard. '*You'll* call a policeman!' he exclaimed. 'If you don't go away, bear, that's just what I intend doing.'

Paddington was a bear with a strong sense of right and wrong and for a moment he stood rooted to the spot looking as if he could hardly believe his eyes, let alone his ears. Then suddenly, before the astonished gaze of the

Browns and everyone else on the hotel terrace, he reached forward and gave the man's beard a determined tug with both paws.

If the other occupants of the hotel were taken aback by the unexpected turn of events the man with the beard was even more upset, and a howl of anguish rang round the terrace as he jumped up clutching his chin.

Paddington's jaw dropped open and a look of alarm came over his face as he examined his empty paws. 'Excuse me,' he exclaimed, raising his hat politely. 'I think I must have made a mistake.'

'A mistake!' spluttered the man, dabbing at his lap with a napkin where a large soup stain had appeared. 'Where's the manager! I want to see the manager. I demand an explanation.'

'I've got an explanation,' said Paddington unhappily, 'but I'm not sure if it's a good one.'

'Oh, crikey,' groaned Jonathan, as a man in a black suit came hurrying on to the scene closely followed by several waiters. 'Here we go again!'

'I've never,' said Mrs Bird, 'met such a bear for getting into hot water. Now what are we going to do?'

Mr Brown sat back in the Brightsea hotel manager's office and stared at Paddington. 'Do you mean to say,' he exclaimed, 'you actually saw a man putting on a false beard behind a pile of deck chairs?'

'There were two of them,' said Paddington importantly. 'I thought I was having a dream and then they went away and I found I was really awake all the time.'

'But I still don't see why you thought it was the man from the *Daily Globe*,' said Mrs Brown.

'I'm afraid this young bear got his "buds" mixed,' said a policeman. 'Quite a natural mistake in the circumstances.'

'You see, he'd stumbled on South Coast Charlie and his pal,' said a second policeman. 'They always call each other "bud". I think they've been seeing too many films on television.'

'South Coast Charlie!' echoed Mrs Bird. 'Goodness me!'

'They tour all the south coast holiday resorts during the summer months doing confidence tricks,' continued the first policeman. 'We've been after them for some time now but they've always kept one step ahead of us. Kept changing their disguises. Thanks to this young bear's description we've a good idea who to look for now. In fact, I daresay there'll be some kind of a reward.'

The Browns looked at one another. After the excitement earlier on, the hotel manager's office seemed remarkably peaceful. Even the man with the beard, now that he had got over his first surprise, looked most impressed by Paddington's explanation. 'I've been mistaken for a few people in my time,' he said, 'but never a Basil Budd let alone a South Coast Charlie.'

'Trust Paddington to find someone with a beard

sitting on the next table,' said Jonathan.

The hotel manager coughed. 'That's not really surprising,' he said. 'There's a magicians' conference on at Brightsea this week and a lot of them are staying at this hotel. You'll see a good many beards.'

'Good gracious!' said Mrs Bird, as she looked through the office window. 'You're quite right. Look at them all!'

The others followed the direction of Mrs Bird's gaze. Now that it had been mentioned there were beards everywhere. Long beards, short ones, whiskery beards and neatly trimmed ones. 'I don't think I've ever seen so many before,' said Mr Brown. 'I suppose that's why South Coast Charlie wore one?'

'That's right, sir,' said one of the policemen. 'It's a good thing this young gentleman didn't try them all. We might have had a nasty scene on our hands.'

'Perhaps you'd care to join me for lunch,' said the man with the beard, addressing the Browns as the policemen stood up to go. 'I'm a magician myself,' he continued, turning to Paddington. 'The Great Umberto. I might even be able to show you a few tricks while we eat.'

'Thank you very much, Mr Umberto,' said Paddington, as the hotel manager hurried on ahead to reserve a table. 'I should like that.'

Altogether Paddington was beginning to think it was a very good day at the sea after all. Although he hadn't managed to win five pounds by confronting Basil Budd he was very keen on tricks and the prospect of having lunch with a real magician sounded most exciting.

'Hmm,' said Mrs Bird, as she followed the others out on to the hotel terrace. 'We may be having lunch with a magician but I have a feeling that even the Great Umberto won't be able to make his meal disappear as quickly as Paddington.'

Paddington pricked up his ears in agreement as he caught Mrs Bird's remark. It was already long past his lunch time and detective work, especially seaside detective work, used up a lot of energy.

'I don't think I shall have many cobwebs left in my whiskers after today, Mr Brown,' he announced amid general agreement, as he sat down at the table to enjoy a well-earned lunch.